Noah & Derek's

ZOOMERS

THE SPEEDY SPIDERSAURUS

Art by *Chris Kennett*

NOVA WEETMAN

Hardie Grant
EGMONT

CHAPTER ONE

As soon as Noah Wriggle hears the front door close he leaps out of bed. Today is **THURSDAY**, Noah's favourite day. On Thursdays his mum and dad both leave early for work. Which means that when his best friend Blue arrives at 7.38 am, they can get started straight away.

Noah dashes down to the kitchen to make some toast before Blue arrives. He chuckles at the sound of his big sister Ellie singing badly in the shower as he spreads butter and jam on three slices.

Noah chews his toast as he gets dressed, then wraps himself up in his dad's old dinner jacket and clears some space at his desk. It's hard to find space anywhere in his room, because it's full of **TREASURE**.

Well, Noah calls it treasure. Ellie calls it **JUNK**, but Noah's pretty sure she's just jealous. Noah never throws anything out. Pieces of string, broken rubber bands, bottle tops - you never know what might come in handy one day.

On Thursdays, Noah is an inventor. But before he can get started, he needs to put on the rest of his inventing outfit.

TOP HAT? ☑ CHECK.

SPOTTED BOW TIE? ☑ CHECK.

GLASSES WITHOUT GLASS? ☑ CHECK.

Noah likes wearing his inventing clothes because it makes him feel like a real inventor. Like his grandfather.

TOP HAT
☑

GLASSES
(WITHOUT GLASS)
☑

SPOTTED
BOW TIE
☑

DAD'S OLD
DINNER JACKET
☑

Now he feels ready.

Noah kneels down and shines a torch over all the stuff under his bed. He spots a broken old toy he'd like to pull apart later. But right now, he has inventing to do. He slides his hand under the bed and pulls out a large, leather-bound, mysterious looking book called **ZOONIVERSE**.

The book once belonged to his grandfather. He gave it to Noah on

his tenth birthday. Tracing the gold lettering on the front, Noah remembers his grandfather explaining the rules of the book. The first is to keep the book hidden. The second is to keep the inventions a secret. And the third is that all inventions must be returned at the end of the day, or the animals will disappear from the book **FOREVER**.

Sitting cross-legged on the floor, Noah checks the time. It's 7.36 am. His skin is all **TINGLY** and he's sure he can hear the book whispering to him, asking him to begin. Surely Blue won't mind if he starts without him.

Noah carefully picks the lock on the side of the book with a hairpin until it pops open. There was a key once, but the Cheetrat swallowed it, so now Noah has to break in like a thief.

As Noah carefully turns the thick cover, the book sighs, like it's breathing. Noah places both his hands on the cover to calm it down, like his grandfather showed him. His chest fills with a fluttering sensation. He lifts out the pair of **DICE**, the special **PENCIL** and the **HOURGLASS** that are tucked into the inside cover just as Blue bursts into the room. Noah jumps, and drops the dice.

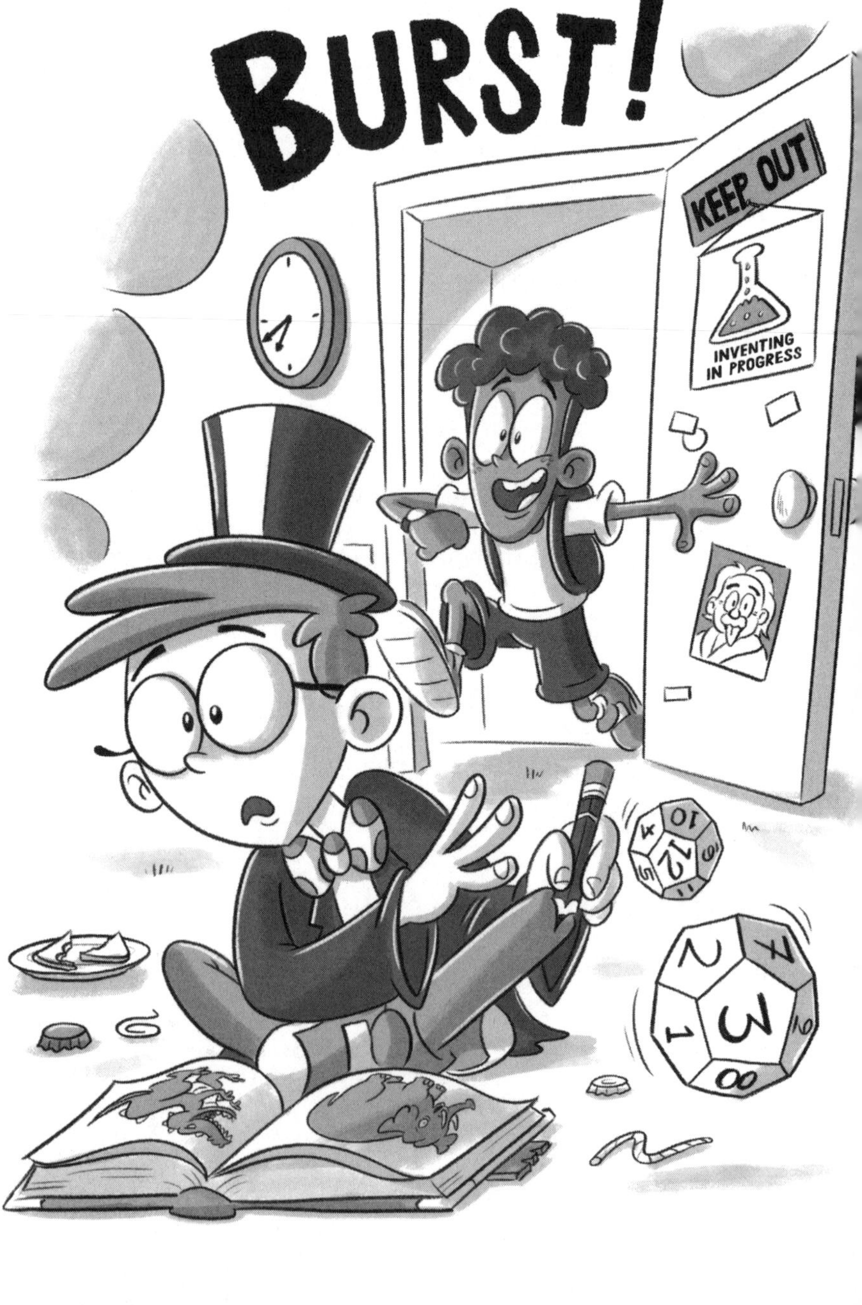
BURST!
KEEP OUT
INVENTING
IN PROGRESS

Blue is wearing his blue school shirt and grey shorts. They don't have to wear a school uniform, but Noah knows that Blue will never wear anything else.

'How come you started without me?!' Blue says, checking his watch.

'I'M NOT LATE! I'M NEVER LATE.'

Noah feels bad. 'I haven't started! I'm just getting it all ready!'

'Good. I'm starving!' says Blue, dropping his schoolbag on the floor.

Noah grins and holds up his plate of half-eaten toast. 'Crusts okay?'

'PERFECT!'

Noah looks around for the two dice he dropped, while Blue gobbles the crusts. Noah is used to Blue eating anything and everything. He's always hungry. Blue says he has a fast metaba - something or other, but Noah secretly thinks Blue is hollow inside.

'Are we going to start?' Blue asks as

soon as he's swallowed the last crust.

Noah reaches under the bed again, feeling around for the missing dice.

'A-ha! It's a six,' he says triumphantly, holding it out to show Blue. While still on his knees, Noah spots the other dice under the cupboard. 'And a four.' He shows Blue the second dice.

'A six and a four. That's page 64,' says Noah, settling back down in front of the book and flipping to the page. But when he spies the eight legs of a large tarantula, he quickly **SLAMS** the book shut.

CHAPTER TWO

'Don't be scared,' says Blue, taking the book and turning back to the page. 'Most **TARANTULAS** are harmless. Some people even keep them as pets.'

'I'm not scared,' Noah says quickly. 'I, er, just have a thing about spiders.'

Noah finds spiders **TERRIFYING**, but he doesn't want to tell Blue that. Blue isn't scared of anything - except failing a test, of course. Which Noah knows would never happen.

'But a pet tarantula would be totally cool!' says Blue.

'Aargh, no! Um, I mean, I don't think Dad would like that.' Noah looks down at the picture. 'It's super hairy.'

'They have special hairs on their stomachs.'

'Like my dad?'

'No. Not unless he can shoot the hairs at his attackers. Like a ninja!'

'Sounds painful,' says Noah.

'Not as painful as what they do to their prey. Their venom **MELTS** flesh. So instead of eating their dinner, they drink it.'

Noah shudders. 'That's disgusting.'

'I like to think of it as a spider's milkshake. Hey, do you have anything else to eat?'

Noah looks around his room. 'Um, there might be a muesli bar in the bookshelf.'

Noah watches Blue ferret through the picture books he can't bear to part with, looking for food. He hopes his friend takes a while - he'd like to avoid the spider for as long as possible.

'Sultanas, ugh,' says Blue, pulling a face at the muesli bar he's found. Noah smiles as Blue unwraps it anyway and starts chewing.

Noah considers suggesting they scrap the spider and roll again. But that would mean admitting just how scared he really is. He peeks again at the hairy creature. Its tiny black beady eyes seem to be staring at him. Noah looks away. He overcame the **RHINOGATOR**, which tried to chew off his legs; surely he can cope with a spider.

'Okay, what's our other animal going to be?' Noah picks up the dice and rolls. 'A one and a five. Page 15,' he says, flicking to the page. A **GREEN TREE FROG** is hanging on a branch.

Blue shakes his head. 'No! That would be a tarantula's dinner. They love drinking frogs. Some spiders even eat birds!'

Noah tries not to think about how big a spider that eats birds would have to be! Instead, he thinks about his new invention. 'Maybe we need something fierce. Quick. Roll again,' says Noah.

Blue tosses the dice into the air.

'A four and a two,' says Blue, flipping through the pages and stopping at a ferocious-looking

TYRANNOSAURUS REX.

'Yes! The **KING** of the tyrant lizards!' cheers Blue. 'That's what the word "Tyrannosaurus" means. I've always wanted to meet one!'

'Well, a T Rex sure is fierce. Should we use it?' Noah asks. He's pretty sure he knows the answer.

'So you're not scared of dinosaurs, even one as fierce as a T Rex, but you are scared of spiders?'

Noah gulps. 'I'm not really scared of them,' he says.

Blue shrugs. 'Remember your **SCREAMS** when the baby spider ran across your arm? You have arachnophobia.'

'Don't call me names!'

'I'm not. It means you're scared of spiders,' says Blue.

'Oh. Right. Well, I'm only a little bit scared. I'm sure I'll be fine.'

CHAPTER THREE

Noah is lying on his stomach drawing the second half of the creature. It already has a tyrannosaurus head, and now Noah is adding the eight spidery legs. He's not enjoying drawing the legs. There are just so many of them, and he keeps imagining how they might feel, **SKATING** across his skin.

Noah is using the special pencil from the *Zooniverse* book. He's not sure, but he thinks maybe the pencil is what makes the magic happen.

'Almost finished?' asks Blue, trying to peek over Noah's shoulder.

'Just drawing all the hairs,' Noah says, frowning with concentration. 'If I miss out on one tiny detail, well, you know ... anything could happen,' he adds, remembering the day he forgot to draw the wings on the Waspmouse and the poor creature **CRASH-LANDED** on the floor.

When Noah has finished the fine

hairs along the legs, he holds up the drawing, hoping Blue will like it as much as he does. **'TA DA!'**

The back half of Noah's creature is a tarantula, and the front half is a T Rex. It has eight spindly legs and a hairy two-part body, two tiny arms, a large tyrannosaurus head, and plenty of teeth.

'That is awesome, Noah!' says Blue, shoving another handful of crusts into his mouth.

'Um ... where did you get *those* crusts?' Noah asks.

'Under the bed.'

Noah shudders. He knows Blue will eat anything, anywhere, anytime - no matter how old it might be - but sometimes he'd rather not watch.

'Okay. Ready to bring our creature to life?' Noah asks, picking up the small hourglass.

'READY!'

Noah holds up the hourglass and turns it slowly until the red sand starts running through the hole. He lies down on his stomach next to Blue, with the drawing between them, and they watch the sand fall. As the last grains drop through, Noah holds his breath. This is his favourite part.

'One potato, two potato, three potato ...' counts Noah. He can barely wait for the potatoes to be counted. Noah feels like everything has stopped. He watches the drawing, waiting until ...

... one hooded eye blinks open and stares up at Noah. Then a hairy leg **POPS FREE** from the page and starts waving around. Noah notices all the tiny hairs starting to stand up. He reaches across and grips Blue's arm. He tries to breathe, but the air gets caught in his throat. There's a small **ROAR** as the creature's head bursts from the page and yawns, revealing rows of shiny teeth.

Noah's eyes widen. He gulps and moves back a little, suddenly worried about this combination. He thought a T Rex head would be **AWESOME**, but now he's not so sure.

'Did you really have to give it so many teeth?' Blue whispers.

'I was trying to make it authentic!' Noah looks at his friend, who has moved back even further.

The rest of the legs pop free from the page, and as the creature steps off the paper, a **SHIMMER** runs along its skin, colouring it. Usually Noah would be delighted at this point, but it's hard to enjoy the moment. There must be a hundred teeth in that mouth.

CHAPTER FOUR

The creature does a little tap dance across the floor, its legs **SKITTERING** wildly like it can't quite control them.

Then it face plants into the floor.
Noah laughs, relieved.

'Oops, I think
it's a bit top
heavy!' says Noah.

DOINK!

'The skull of a T Rex can be up to
1.5 metres long,' says Blue. 'But usually
it has a tail to balance its head. Maybe
you should have added one.'

Noah frowns. 'Maybe she just needs
a bit of help learning to walk. Like a
baby calf does when it's born,' says
Noah. He's hoping he's right, and that
Blue, for once, is wrong.

It doesn't look quite so scary now.

Noah reaches down to scoop the creature up, just as she swings around and opens her mouth, latching onto his finger. Noah **YELPS**, then starts giggling.

'Lucky that special pencil is a bit blunt - her teeth aren't that sharp,' he tells Blue as the creature sucks on his finger.

'Very lucky,' nods Blue wisely. 'The T Rex was a meat eater. It probably had the strongest bite of any animal that ever lived.' Blue chomps his teeth fiercely to make his point. 'Its front teeth **GRIPPED**, its side teeth **RIPPED**, and its back teeth **DICED**.'

'WOW! GRIP, RIP, DICE!' repeats Noah, looking down at his forefinger, which the creature is now chewing. It sort of tickles.

Noah is suddenly relieved that he drew this meat-eater at such a small size. 'So what should we call her?' he asks Blue.

'Hmm,' Blue moves closer to get a better look at the little creature in Noah's hand. Still biting at Noah's finger, she fixes her yellow T Rex eyes on Blue. She waves her two little T Rex arms and lifts two spider legs.

Blue's face lights up. 'Look! She's saying hello!' A second later, the creature bares her teeth and roars ferociously. Blue **JOLTS** back in alarm. Noah can't hide his laughter.

Blue recovers quickly and grins broadly at Noah. 'So cool!' he says. 'How about we call her "Tyrannarantula"?'

The little creature clamps onto

Noah's finger again.

'Good name,' says Noah, 'but it's a bit hard to say.' He thinks hard. 'How about ... Spidersaurus!' he announces proudly. '**SPIDEY** for short?'

'I like it!'

Noah pulls his finger free and helps the Spidersaurus stand. Her eight legs scatter again in various directions, like she's dancing, but she manages to stay upright this time.

'We might need to feed her,' says Blue. 'She needs meat.'

'There's a ham sandwich in my lunch,' suggests Noah.

But they're interrupted by a bang on the door. It's Ellie. 'School time, boys,' she calls. Ellie always walks them to school on Thursdays.

'Coming,' shouts Noah.

Noah tucks Spidey deep into the pocket of his dad's jacket, where he can keep an eye on her. He pats her scaly head with his fingers. There's a muffled **ROAR**, followed by a **PURR**.

'I think she likes having her head scratched,' says Noah, smiling.

The boys grab their schoolbags and step out into the hall just as Ellie goes to open the bedroom door.

She takes a suspicious look.

'What are you two up to?' asks Ellie.

'Nothing. Why do you always ask that?' says Noah.

'Because you're wearing your inventing glasses, and you just answered my **QUESTION** with another **QUESTION**.'

Noah forgot to take his glasses off. He tucks them into his other pocket and smiles at his sister innocently.

'Better?' he says.

'Yep, but I still think you're up to something,' she says. 'And you can't wear that jacket to school.'

'Yes I can. It's comfortable.'

'It's too big. And it's Dad's.'

'He doesn't mind. I always wear it on Thursdays,' Noah says without thinking. **'WHY THURSDAYS?'** Ellie asks.

'Because Blue likes it,' says Noah, shooting Blue a look.

'I do. I really like it,' says Blue.

Giving up, Ellie puts her headphones on and heads down the hall. Blue nudges Noah and says, 'I'm not sure it's a good idea to take the Spidersaurus to school.'

'It'll be fine,' says Noah confidently. 'I'll keep my hand in my pocket so she can't escape.' But his friend doesn't look so sure.

'Um, Noah, remember what happened when you took the **DUCKAPOTOMOUS** to school?' Blue says in a loud whisper as they follow Ellie out the front door.

Noah looks at his friend and grins. 'I don't think I could ever forget that day!'

CHAPTER FIVE

Waving goodbye to Ellie, Noah and Blue hurry in through the school gates. There are kids everywhere. The boys head to their lockers.

'I'll leave Spidey in my locker until lunchtime,' says Noah. 'That way she can't get up to any mischief.'

'Good plan,' says Blue.

When the boys reach their lockers, Noah gives Spidey a reassuring pat, then tries to pull his hand out of his pocket. But he can't.

'BLUE, I'M STUCK,' says Noah in a loud whisper.

'What do you mean, stuck?'

Noah pulls and pulls and finally yanks his hand out of his pocket. It's covered in a thick spider web. Noah yelps and tries to shake the sticky web from his hand, but it won't come off. 'I hate spider webs,' he says, frantically wiping his hands on his locker door.

'Spidey's just making herself at home,' says Blue, peering inside Noah's pocket. 'Tarantulas don't spin webs to catch prey, like other spiders do. They spin homes for comfort.'

Noah frowns. 'Blue, it's not comfortable *for me* having a spider web in my pocket! How do I get the Spidersaurus out?'

'I DON'T KNOW,' says Blue.

Noah looks at his friend, shocked. 'But Blue, you know everything.'

'Technically not **EVERYTHING!** I do know that a tarantula's body is like a **SILK-SPINNING** factory.

They have special glands that make silk - they can produce five or six different types, for different uses.'

'But that doesn't help me get her out of my pocket!'

The school bell sounds and kids rush towards the classroom.

'I also know that's the school bell,' says Blue, cheekily. 'That means class is about to start. And that means you'll just have to take off your jacket and leave it in your locker.'

'But it's cold! I only have a T-shirt on underneath.'

Blue nods. 'I know.'

'And it's my dad's special jacket!'

'I know. But Noah, we can't take the Spidersaurus to class.'

Just at that moment their teacher, Mr Davy, walks past wearing his wide morning smile and carrying a large pile of books.

'READY FOR CLASS, BOYS?'

ZOOP

'Almost,' says Noah.

'EVERYTHING OKAY, NOAH?' Mr Davy asks.

'Everything's fine, Mr Davy,' says Noah in a very small voice.

'Great. Then I'll see you in class in a second,' he says, and heads for the classroom.

'It's okay, Noah,' Blue whispers urgently. 'We'll find a way to get the Spidersaurus out of your pocket later on. **I PROMISE!**'

Reluctantly, Noah slips his dad's dinner jacket off and makes it into a cosy little bed in his locker. Then he carefully closes the locker door and follows Blue to class. Noah really hopes that Spidey is going to be okay in his locker. And that his dad's jacket is going to survive whatever Spidey might do to it!

CHAPTER SIX

Noah sits next to Blue in class like he always does. He keeps one eye on what they're doing and the other on the clock, counting the minutes until he can check on Spidey. As usual, Blue has his pencil ready to go, and is staring at Mr Davy, listening attentively.

Noah is amazed that Blue can concentrate on schoolwork at a time like this.

'All right everyone, that's it for this class,' says Mr Davy as the bell goes. Like a **FLASH**, Noah grabs his books and runs out to the hallway. He doesn't have time to wait for Blue. Sometimes he likes to stay behind and sharpen all his pencils, ready for the next class.

When Blue finally arrives, Noah is desperately trying to open his locker. 'Weird, my locker's **JAMMED**,' he says.

'Let me help,' says Blue.

Together the boys grab the handle
and start pulling. Straining, they finally
YANK it open to find it full of
spider webs.

Noah gulps. Everything is white and
puffy, like a **CLOUD** has been squashed
into his locker.

'Wow … Spidey has been busy,' says Blue, his eyes wide.

'She sure has.'

Noah stares into his locker. 'Where do you think she is?' he asks.

'I don't know,' says Blue.

'How will we find her? I can't put my hand in that!'

'Yes you can. Pretend it's fairy floss - just don't try to eat it,' says Blue.

Noah closes his eyes and imagines he's touching fairy floss. He reaches carefully into the dense spider web and fumbles around with his hand. He starts to panic. 'Spidey's not in here!'

He pulls the jacket out through the web and checks the pockets. Nothing.

'SHE'S GONE!' hisses Noah, looking wildly around the hallway for any sign of her.

Blue is peering into Noah's locker. 'Her teeth might be blunt, but they can still bite through metal. Look!'

Noah takes a cautious look, not wanting to get too close to the cloud. He sees that a jagged hole has been chewed in the back.

'WHOA!'

'Scientists think that an adult T Rex could bite through a car,' says Blue.

'Maybe you should have mentioned that fact a little earlier!'

'It's not so bad. At least she didn't bite your finger like that.'

'Where can she be?'

Noah's question is answered by a noise like the sounds of **SCREECHING** tyres, fingernails being **DRAGGED** down a blackboard and a fork **SLIDING** on a china plate, all put together ... and then turned up really loud. All around Noah, kids scream and cover their ears. The sound seems to be coming from everywhere.

SCREEEEEEEEECHH!

And then it stops.

'What was that?' whispers Noah, feeling a wave of **DREAD** twist through his tummy.

But before Blue can answer there is another high-pitched screeching sound. Only this time it's coming from Mr Davy, who is yelling into a megaphone.

'Alright everyone, outside, everyone assemble on the sports oval. Come on, out, out, out!' he shouts.

Noah and Blue have no choice but to follow the other kids outside.

Noah starts biting his nails. Could that awful racket be Spidey on the loose? The **TERRIFYING SCREECH** rings out again. Blue looks at Noah. Noah looks at Blue.

Then the sound stops. Blue leans close to Noah. 'It's Spidey, isn't it?'

Noah nods. 'I think that might be the noise a T Rex makes when it's trapped.'

CHAPTER SEVEN

As Noah and Blue follow everyone out to the oval, Blue asks, 'What's going on, Mr Davy?'

'Possum stuck in the roof, I expect,' says Mr Davy. 'But the principal wants everyone outside just in case.'

'I don't think possums sound like that, Mr Davy,' says Noah. He's almost ready to tell Mr Davy the truth.

'It's okay boys. They've called an **EXTERMINATOR** to come and get rid of it, whatever it is,' says Mr Davy. He turns to round up some stragglers, calling their names through his megaphone.

'What's an exterminator, Blue?' asks Noah.

'Someone who gets rid of pests,' explains Blue, looking worried.

'BUT SPIDEY ISN'T A PEST!' Noah feels his heart start to race.

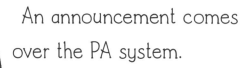

An announcement comes over the PA system.

'ALL STUDENTS ARE TO WAIT ON THE OVAL UNTIL FURTHER NOTICE.'

All around them, kids are trying to guess what the sound could be.

'What are we going to do?' asks Blue.

'We have to find Spidey before the exterminator does. Quick, follow me,' says Noah, shuffling casually through the crowd.

'Now what?' whispers Blue.

'We'll have to go around the long way and go in from the front,' says Noah.

He looks around to make sure no-one is watching. But the teachers are all too busy chatting about the noise to notice what they're up to.

'OKAY ... GO!' whispers Noah.

Both boys scurry as fast as their legs can take them. When they reach the front gate, Blue stops.

'Um, Noah, we're not allowed to leave the school grounds,' says Blue.

'Blue, just think what will happen if the exterminator catches Spidey. Aren't you prepared to get in trouble to save her life?'

'I don't say this often, but you're right!'

Noah grins at his best friend. 'Okay, follow me.' They bolt out of the gate, race down a side street and then double back, finding themselves huffing and puffing at the front doors of the school.

'Look!' cries Blue, pointing to the car park.

A van is pulling in. There's a giant rubber cockroach on top of it, and on the side, in bold letters, are the words **'ERICA THE EPIC EXTERMINATOR.'**

'Hurry,' says Noah, pushing Blue through the front doors. As they burst into the hallway, Noah stops dead and Blue crashes into him.

'Oh no …' says Noah, gazing around in horror. The entire hallway is covered from floor to ceiling in thick spider webs. 'I really hate spider webs.'

'Wow! Our Spidersaurus is amazing!' says Blue.

Just then the **SCREECHING** starts again. Blue covers his ears.

'It's even louder now. It sounds like it's coming from the science room!' says Noah.

'Huh?' shouts Blue.

Noah lifts Blue's hands from his ears. 'I said, it sounds like it's coming from the science room!'

'Oh. Okay. Let's go!' Blue grabs Noah's arm and **CHARGES** headfirst into the thick spider web, **DRAGGING** Noah behind him. Webs are sticking to his hair and his clothes, and he can't wipe them away fast enough. He really wants to find Spidey, but it feels like his courage is tangled in spider webs, too.

CHAPTER EIGHT

As they reach the science room, Noah catches sight of their reflection. They are completely covered in webs. They don't even look human anymore. They look like Egyptian **MUMMIES**.

Noah tries to take a step towards the classroom door, but his legs won't move properly.

He looks down and sees, to his horror, that they are bound together with webs. Noah starts ripping until he has freed one leg, and then the other. Finally he can move.

Blue has his hand on the door to the science room when Noah hears the main door swing open, followed by the sound of heavy footsteps. The boys freeze and stare at each other.

There's a loud, booming voice. 'Come out, come out, wherever you are!'

'Does she mean us?' whispers Blue, his eyes wide.

Noah wipes the last of the webs

from his face. 'No. I think she's talking to the possum.'

'You mean Spidey?'

Noah nods. 'Yeah. Come on.'

They **SNEAK** into the science room and hide behind the door. Noah holds a finger to his lips and listens. He can hear something on the roof. He points to the window, and together the boys slide it open. Noah sticks his head out and looks up. There's a woman in overalls on the roof. She's spraying something from what looks like a gun.

Noah waits until she's gone past the window and then signals to Blue to start searching the room. They look in corners and in cupboards, and even behind the poster of the periodic table.

'Where would a Spidersaurus hide?' Noah asks, peering over the top of a beaker.

'A tropical rainforest or an arid desert.'

'Blue, we're in the science lab,' says Noah.

'You asked. Those are the correct habitats for a tarantula and a T Rex.'

Noah knows better than to argue. Instead, he leans under a table and spots a **DADDY-LONG-LEGS** trying to spin a very small web around a fly. It gives Noah an idea.

'We need to lure it with something,' says Noah.

'Good idea. See if you can find something to draw it out. I'm just going to go and grab my lunch!' says Blue.

'How can you think about food at a time like this?' says Noah, shaking his head. 'Spidey's life is in danger!'

'But my locker's just across the corridor ... and I'm starving!' says Blue with a shrug as he ducks out of the classroom and disappears.

Noah waits for Blue to tiptoe to his locker, grab his lunch and tiptoe back again. Noah shuts the door behind him just as the **SCREECHING** starts again.

'Where's it coming from?' says Noah.

But Blue is too busy inspecting his lunch to answer. 'Oh no, not meatloaf sandwiches again! Dad promised me tuna!' he says glumly.

'Did you say meatloaf?' cries Noah.

'Yep.'

'Perfect!' Without waiting, Noah snatches Blue's sandwich and takes the meatloaf out. Normally he would never try to take Blue's food. He knows better.

'HEY!' cries Blue. 'That's my meatloaf!'

'You don't even like meatloaf.'

'I know, but it's still food.'

'Too bad. Spidey needs it more than you do!'

Noah scuttles to the back of the science room and peeps through the door into the next room.

'The screech sounded like it came from this direction. Come on,' says Noah.

Noah waits while Blue quickly eats the bread from his now-empty sandwich, then they head through the door, leaving a long trail of spider webs behind them.

CHAPTER NINE

Noah and Blue scurry into the art room. It's dark and quiet. Noah flicks the light on.

'You check down the front and I'll look up the back,' he tells Blue. 'We're going to use the meatloaf to lure her out. So **PLEASE** don't eat it!'

Noah rips the meatloaf in two, passes

half to Blue, then starts searching.

'There's nothing here,' whispers Blue
'There aren't even any webs.'

Noah can't see any sign of Spidey either. Suddenly he finds himself looking at an art project. It's a great big diorama, complete with miniature palm trees, volcanos and plastic dinosaurs. And there, hiding behind one of the little volcanoes, is Spidey, chewing the head of a plastic diplodocus.

Noah waves a little piece of meatloaf at her. Spidey scurries over the volcano and gobbles it all up!

'Blue! I've found her!' whispers Noah, reaching out to scoop up the Spidersaurus.

But just as Noah is about to grab her, the door bursts open and a waft of gas enters, followed by the exterminator!

Noah freezes.

'WHATAREYOUKIDSDOINGINHERE? YOU'REMEANTTOBEONTHEOVAL!'

roars the exterminator.

Confused, Noah and Blue look at each other.

'Pardon?' says Noah.

The exterminator takes off her gas mask and repeats, 'What are you kids doing in here? You're meant to be on the oval!'

Noah steps forward. 'Oh, well, we were locked in and couldn't get out. You saved us!'

Noah smiles one of his biggest smiles - the kind he uses on his mum when she's caught him pulling something apart.

'Oh, you poor things. Don't mind the

smell, it's just tea tree oil - possums hate it. Sorry if I gave you a fright.'

'That's okay. Have you caught the possum yet?' asks Noah. As he speaks, he spies a **FLASH** of movement as the Spidersaurus dashes across the diorama. Alarmed, Blue looks at Noah. Noah looks at Blue. Noah stares pointedly at the meatloaf in Blue's hand, willing him to get the hint.

Blue looks confused for a moment, then his frown disappears. He **TOSSES** his meatloaf into the air. Noah catches it and **SLAMS** it into his pocket.

The Spidersaurus sniffs the air and races towards Noah's pocket. The exterminator takes a step forward just as Noah turns around, holding his pocket open, and the Spidersaurus leaps in. Noah turns back to face the exterminator.

'WHAT WAS THAT?'

she asks, taking a step towards Noah.

'What was what?' says Noah with an even bigger smile, backing away.

'I saw something running. It looked strange!'

'Was it this?' Noah reaches down and snatches up the plastic dinosaur. Its head drops to one side where the Spidersaurus has chewed it.

'No. It seemed to be moving,' says the exterminator, scratching her head.

'That'd be the tea tree oil. Too much tea tree oil can make you see things,' says Blue.

If Noah didn't know better, he'd think Blue just made that up.

The exterminator sniffs the air. 'Really?'

'I remember reading something about it,' says Blue.

'Huh. Never had a problem before,' she says.

'Anyway, we'd better get back to the oval,' says Noah.

He grabs Blue by the arm and pulls him from the room.

'Good luck with the, er ... **POSSUM**,' says Noah, heading out of the room.

'I'm not so sure it is a possum,' says the exterminator. 'Did you see the giant web in the hallway? Never seen anything like it!'

Noah **DRAGS** Blue out of the room and they **RACE** back the way they came, through the front door, around the block, down the side street and in through the gate. Then they **SNEAK** back to the sports oval.

'That was close,' says Noah as they plonk down a safe distance from the other kids. 'Was that true about the tea tree oil?'

'I don't know.'

'You lied?'

'I know what Spidey means to you, Noah,' says Blue.

Noah smiles at his friend. He can't believe Blue lied to **PROTECT** Spidey. 'She must mean a lot to you too.'

'Yeah. I guess.' Then Blue peers into Noah's pocket. 'I hope she liked my meatloaf,' says Blue.

'I'm sure she did. Thanks, Blue. You can share my sandwiches,' says Noah.

'A full-size T Rex could eat up to 230 kilos in one bite!'

'That's a lot of meatloaf,' says Noah.

CHAPTER TEN

Hunched over so nobody can see what they are doing, Noah and Blue are sitting under a tree, **WRESTLING** with Spidey over a stick. Noah wonders if she's sharpening her teeth, then shoves the thought away.

Noah spies the exterminator coming outside to talk to Mr Davy. He elbows Blue and points. The exterminator is shrugging a lot, and shaking her head. Then Mr Davy nods.

'Okay everyone, all clear. Back inside!' he shouts.

'Is it lunchtime yet, Noah?' asks Blue.

As if Mr Davy has heard him, he calls out, 'Back to class everyone. Lunch will be a bit late today.'

Blue looks miserable. Then he remembers the rest of the meatloaf in his pocket. He's about to eat it when Noah snatches it from his hand.

'STOP TAKING MY FOOD!'

Blue exclaims.

'We need that to make sure Spidey isn't hungry in class. We don't want her **SCREECHING** again!'

'I'm so hungry *I* might start screeching!'

Outside their classroom, Noah sees Mr Davy holding a ladder. The sports teacher is balanced on top, trying to reach the last of the spider webs. Mr Davy looks at Noah and Blue.

'Boys, any idea who thought it would be funny to fill the school with fake spider webs?'

'NO,' says Noah.

'DEFINITELY NOT,'

adds Blue, as Noah brushes a scrap of spider web from Blue's hair.

They share a tiny smile.

CHAPTER ELEVEN

Noah follows Ellie into the house, with Blue close behind. Suddenly there's a sad, **RUMBLING**, screeching kind of sound.

'What is it, little one?' asks Noah, looking into his pocket.

'Um, that was actually my stomach, Noah,' says Blue. 'Can I have some toast?'

'Sure thing, Blue,' says Noah.

While Blue eats, Noah reaches into his pocket to take out the Spidersaurus.

'Ow! I think her teeth are getting sharper,' he says, pulling his hand out of his pocket. The Spidersaurus is attached to his finger.

'Maybe she's hungry too?' Blue says.

Noah opens the fridge to look for some meat. He finds a cooked lamb chop and puts it on a plate. Spidey **LEAPS** onto the chop and starts attacking it like it's still alive. Within seconds, all that's left is a bone.

NOM

NOSH

CHOMP

SLOBBER

'Wow! That was fast,' says Blue, sounding impressed.

'Even faster than you,' says Noah, scooping up Spidey and patting her **SCALY** head. She rolls onto her back so Noah can rub her tummy.

'Time to say goodbye?' asks Blue.

Noah nods. 'Yep. Have to let her go soon or the T Rex and the tarantula will disappear forever from the book, and then they can never visit again.'

Blue stacks up all the toast crusts. 'I'll keep these for the morning.' He lifts his schoolbag onto his shoulder. Blue never likes saying goodbye to their creatures.

'See ya, Blue.'

Noah waits for Blue to go, then carries Spidey to his bedroom. Holding her with one hand so she can't wander off, he struggles into his inventing gear with the other. Then he takes the book out from under the bed and turns to find the faint outline of his drawing wedged between the pages of the book.

Noah places Spidey gently onto the page and smiles as she **FACE PLANTS** one last time. As she settles into place, a little haze of **DUST** falls around her and runs along the lines of Noah's original drawing.

'Bye, Spidey,' says Noah. He closes his eyes and shuts the book.

'One potato, two potato, three potato,' he whispers.

Then he opens the book and checks the page, smiling when he sees the tarantula back where it should be. It doesn't look so scary anymore.

He checks that the T Rex has made

it back too, tracing his finger across the rows of sharp teeth. He slides the book back under his bed then takes off his top hat, his bow tie and his glasses.

Then he slips his arms from his dad's dinner jacket and hangs it on the back of the door, ready for **NEXT** Thursday morning.

THE END

MEET THE TEAM

NOVA WEETMAN wrote her first book at age 12. A dystopian story about jelly eating, it's predictably unpublished. From there,  she wrote for TV shows like *Pixel Pinkie*, *H2O*, and *Fanshaw and Crudnut*, before returning to the thing she loves most - writing books for kids. Now she writes YA novels, middle fiction and junior fiction.

CHRIS KENNETT is a children's author and illustrator. He's illustrated several books for kids, including *Pixel Raiders*, *Star Wars: Aliens, Creatures and Beasts* and *Alpha Monsters*. He's also illustrated for the TV adaptation of *The Day My Butt Went Psycho*.

COLLECT MORE ZOONIVERSE ADVENTURES!

Noah & Blue's ZOONIVERSE THE SPEEDY SPIDERSAURUS
NOVA WEETMAN

Noah & Blue's ZOONIVERSE THE OUTSTANDING OCTOKEY
NOVA WEETMAN

Noah & Blue's ZOONIVERSE THE MARVELLOUS MOLEON
NOVA WEETMAN

Noah & Blue's ZOONIVERSE THE TUMBLING TIGERDILLO
NOVA WEETMAN

FOR ARLO, WHO'S FOREVER PULLING TREASURES OUT OF HIS HAT. – NOVA

FOR TRACEY. FOR SPOTTING MY TALENTS EARLY ON. LOVE YOU SIS, XXX. – CHRIS

Noah and Blue's Zooniverse: The Speedy Spidersaurus
published in 2019 by Hardie Grant Egmont
Ground Floor, Building I, 658 Church Street
Richmond, Victoria 3121, Australia
www.hardiegrantegmont.com

Text copyright © 2019 Nova Weetman
Illustrations copyright © Chris Kennett
Series copyright © 2019 Hardie Grant Egmont
Series design by Kristy Lund-White

A catalogue record for this
book is available from the
National Library of Australia

Printed in Australia by McPherson's Printing Group,
Maryborough, Victoria.

10 9 8 7 6 5 4 3 2 1

MIX
Paper from
responsible sources
FSC® C001695
www.fsc.org

The paper in this book is FSC® certified.
FSC® promotes environmentally responsible,
socially beneficial and economically viable
management of the world's forests.